"Revolting . . ."
— *The New Messes*

"The geeks have a word for it . . ."
—*Newsfreak*

"Brings up the indigestable . . ."
— *Gourmand* Magazine

"Towards more pig-grotesque speech . . ."
—*The Reader's Disgust*

"I hate to gush, but . . . whoop!"
—John Upchuck

"We hope this one isn't released silently."
—*The Heinie Report*

"The offal truth . . ."
—*Butchers' Paper*

"Lucky we didn't step in it . . ."
—*Dog Walkers' Daily*

". . . Good, though!"
—*Hunters' World*

"Digs deep . . . In excellent taste."
— *The Ghoul Guide's Handbook*

"Flush with success . . ."
—*Harper's Pissoir*

"Long awaited and most welcome . . ."
— *Times of the Month*

# grosseries

(groh-sur-eez)

*n.:* the proper words for improper things; names for the all-too-common objects and events that totally barf you out.

## Sean Kelly and Trish Todd

*with pen and oink drawings by*
**Rick Meyerowitz**

ST. MARTIN'S PRESS / NEW YORK

grosseries

Copyright © 1987 by Sean Kelly and Trish Todd

Library of Congress Catalog Card Number: 87-50344

ISBN: 0-312-90767-2     Can. ISBN: 0-312-90768-0

Printed in the United States of America

First St. Martin's Press mass market edition/July 1987

10 9 8 7 6 5 4 3 2 1

**We gruntfully acknowledge the contributions of the following:**

Dolores McAuliffe

Dominick Anfuso

Harry Choron

Sandy Choron

William J. Elliston, Jr.

William J. Elliston, III

Nancy Goodman

Ron Hauge

Bill Irvine

Chris Kelly

Rory Kelly

Mitchell Kriegman

Gary Luke

Elaine Pfefferblit

Charlie Rubin

Louis B. Todd, Jr.

Louis B. Todd, III

Patricia C. Todd

Rosie Trickett

### adieu-doo
(ahd-yoo-du) *n.:* the sentimental impulse to look back into the toilet

### afterburp
(ah-ftur-berp) *n.:* residual, highly acidic taste persisting in the mouth following a bout of either regur-gitation or "yurk"ing (which See)

### aqualungers
(ah-kwah-luhn-gurz) *n. pl.:* slimy, phlemlike organisms lurking between pebbles in shallow water, which lust to seep into the spaces between human toes

### arselife

(ahrs-lyf) *n.:* unit of thermal time-measurement, with special reference to the duration of anonymous residual body heat on bar stools and bus and toilet seats

### arugalooze

(aroo-gah-looz) *n.:* semi-gelatinous brown liquid invariably located in the back corners of a refrigerator's "vegetable crisper" drawer

# bellitosis

(bel-it-oh-sis) *n.:* the smell peculiar
to the mouthpiece of a public
telephone

### blood swat

(blud swaht) *n.:* the scarlet Rorschach left on the wall memorializing the execution of a full mosquito

### boogeroid

(booh-gur-oyd) *n.:* clot of nasal mucus so substantial it must be brought down the back stairs and made to exit via the mouth

### bowlover

(bohl-oh-oh-vur) *n.:* brief moment of certainty that the toilet is about to back up

### bowser-trouser

(bow-zer trow-zer) *n.*: white-ish sticky condition of pants legs subsequent to encounter with rutting male canine

## brillage

(bril-idj) *n.:* indelible shit-colored stains left on sink enamel by ancient scouring pads

## broll

(brawl) *n.:* the yellowish brown blob of coagulated grease commonly found on the surface of broiled burgers and steaks. "Just scrape the broll off when Harry's not looking."

## bumgulp

(buhm-guhlp) *v.:* to repress, by reabsorption, a passage of gas. Compare: "yurk"

## cacaracha

(kah-kah-rah-tsha) *n.:* roach doo-doo

## cannisterd

(kan-is-turd) *n.:* brownish-black microbe-hosting glob of grot immediately adjacent to the unpopped top of the last beer or soda in the fridge

## caramelites

(kahr-mel-itz) *n.:* community of
wriggling grubs revealed when a
very old candy bar is unwrapped

## carrie-over

(kahr-ee oh-vur) *n.:* warped,
wet-cornered paper match book,
commonly occurring on snack bar
tables; evidently employed by
previous owner as a tool of dental
hygiene

# chewticle

(tshew-tik-uhl) *n.:* the edible parts of the human finger, around and beneath the fingernail

### chow poo yuk

(tchow poow yukh) *n.:* the overwhelmingly pungent odor of a Chinese restaurant washroom

### clammygam

(clam-mee gahm) *n.:* surprisingly moist, sticky condition of the back of the thighs after rising from a public toilet seat

# clinge

(klinj) *v. intr.:* to shudder in revulsion at the sound of someone publicly clipping finger- or toenails

### Coney Island whitefish

(cohn-ee eye-land wyt fish) *n.:* used condom discarded in a public place. "There's a Coney Island whitefish stuck to your shoe."

### cradle scarf

(kray-duhl skarf) *n.:* substance found between the fleshy folds under a baby's chin; like cradle cap, but moister and smellier

### crappie
(krah-pee) *n.:* half-submerged
disintegrating diaper encountered
while swimming

### crimscum
(krim-skuhm) *v.:* to leave a greasy
scarlet smear on the rim of a glass or
cup by means of lipstick

# crudlery

(kruhd-luhr-ee) *n.*: yellowing-green substance on restaurant knives, forks, and spoons; resistant to attempts at removal by thumbnail, spit-upon table napkin, etc.

## crustocean

(krust-oshun) *adj.:* of or relating to shellfish stool, e.g., the horrifying green slime inside lobsters, shrimp veins, crayfish bowels, etc. Compare: "guppygrot"

## cudsnap

(kuhd-snahp) *v. intr.:* to emit astoundingly loud, wet cracking and popping sounds by chewing gum

## dandrifts

(dan-driftz) *n.:* small mounds and reefs of tiny dry white flakes on library reading tables over which professorial types have pondered while vigorously scratching their beards

## dermie crisps

(durm-ee kryspz) *n. pl.:* edible strips of peeling sunburn

## deweys

(doo-eez) *n. pl.:* whatever anonymously applied goo keeps the odd pages of library books stuck together

## diaphlegm

(dy-ah-flem) *n.:* postcoital drip

## discustard

(dis-kus-turd) *n.:* the particularly indelible orange grunge surrounding the bolts that fasten the toilet to the bathroom floor. "It's going to take a sandblaster to get rid of this discustard."

## doggyfog

(daw-gee-fawg) *n.:* wisps of steam rising from the freshly produced puppy poop you have thoughtfully scooped and are in the act of transporting by hand to the corner trash basket

## down-chuck

(downn tsh-uhk) *v.:* to re-ingest
vomit at the last possible moment.
Compare: "bumgulp"

### ear muffins

(eer muf-nz) *n. pl.:* tufts of unruly hair sprouting from the ears of elderly gentlemen

### eggs derelict

(ehgz dare-a-licked) *n.:* a plate of unfinished breakfast that has been used as an ashtray

### ejack o'late

(ee-jak-oh-layte) *n.*: copious liquid discharge occurring in the bottom of a flaccid Halloween pumpkin on or about November 2

### filther tips

(fill-thur tipz) *n. pl.:* unsightly and smelly orange-stained thumb and index fingers of chain smokers; early symptom of lung disease

### filum

(fyl-uhm) *n.:* the tacky, sticky stuff on the floors of movie theaters; in "adult" movie theaters also finds its way onto seat backs, into patrons' hair.

### flopdrizzle

(flawp-dri-zul) *n.:* the sound from the next stall

## fluzey

(floo-zee) *adj.:* the smell inside last
year's woolen ski mask, this year

## foulicles

(fowl-lick-uhls) *n. pl.:* sweat-matted
nest of underarm hair; frequently
displayed at basketball games, nude
beaches

# freezer farts

(free-zur fah-tz) *n. pl.:* stinky ice
cubes

## fumunda

(fuh-mun-dah) *n.:* "toe jam" extracted not from between the toes, but "from under" them

## fungass

(fuhn-gas) *n.:* white, wrinkled mushroomoid condition of the buttocks; consequence of sitting around too long in wet swim suit

## gaffergum

(gahf-ur-guhm) *v.:* to suck, click, pop, or rattle the dentures

## galoosh

(gahl-oosh) *n.:* puddles and shoals of thick black glistening slop on the floors of all vehicles (e.g., trains, buses, cars) during the snowy season

## gargyles

(gahr-gile-z) *n. pl.:* socks which, when flung halfway up a wall, stick there

### gilletanous

(djil-eht-ehn-us) *adj.*: of or pertaining to the fuzzy damp material accumulating between twin blades of a razor

### gnawsea

(noz-see-awe) *n.*: queasy feeling evoked while watching a stranger or loved one attempt to chew off a callus, wart, or corn

### greensneak

(green-sneek) *v.:* to surreptitiously dispose of freshly snagged nasal mucus units by wiping them on or sticking them to the undersurface of chairs or other furniture. *n.:* person who would do such a thing

### guppygrot
(guh-pee-grawt) *n.:* slippery black strings and flakes befouling the bottom of fishbowls and aquariums. Compare: "crustocean"

### gutchas
(guht-tschuz) *n. p.:* bug bits stuck to a flyswatter

### gutter gravy
(guh-tur gray-vee) *n.:* rich, full-bodied servings of curbside puddle slop spewed on the legs of pedestrians by the tires of passing cars

## hairyola

(hayr-ee-oh-la) *n.:* nipple hair

## hamperfunk

(ham-per-phunk) *n.:* aroma, reminiscent of low tide, arising from long neglected laundry

# handkerchoo

(han-kur-tchoo) *v. intr.:* to sneeze
directly into the cupped palms

## hanus

(hein-ous) *adj.:* Of or similar to male buttock cleavage; inches of utterly unappealing ass-crevasse looming into view above the belt line when the owner bends or squats. Syn.: déculeté

## hock-boggle

(hawk-baw-gul) *v.:* to stare in morbid fascination at a drop of your own saliva contributed to the lapel of your conversational partner, himself or herself so far blissfully unaware of same

## hopswill

(hawp-swil) *n.:* mysterious liquid, pisslike in color and odor, that saturates paper bag of empties you are returning — and your clothes. Compare: "dregful"

# howdy-dew

(how-dee-doo) *n.:* drop of moisture
clinging to the weenie-tip after
late-night pee; invariably transferred
to flank of sleeping mate

## iccough

(ick-up) *See* "yerk"

## idiot's lunch

(ihd-ee-otz luh-tsh) *n.:* dry or moist nasal mucus patiently gathered, joyfully ingested. Of little nutritional value, but inexpensive and readily available

## iguano

(ihg-wah-no) *n.:* substance on the bottom of a terrarium

## incontinents

(ihn-kohn-tin-ense) *n. pl.:* weirdly maplike stains on mattresses

## instink

(in-stink) *n.:* the atavistic urge among dogs to attempt, by pitiful scratching, the burial of their droppings in concrete

## jacknasties

(jak-nah-steez) *n. pl.:* stiff wads of facial tissue beneath the beds of adolescent boys

## jacooze

(j'accuse) *n.:* clotted swirls of mucoid scuzz rising to and drifting upon the surface of a hot tub

## jackson bollocks

(jax-un bawl-ox) *n.:* brightly colored variegated scrotal rash

## javacurdle

(jah-vah kerd-uhl) *n.:* constellation of sour milk or cream swirling on the surface of coffee

# jazzim

(jah-zym) *n.:* copious gouts of fluid
shaken and spilled out of horn
player's instrument between solos

### jock hitch

(jawk hitch) *v.*: to adjust the family jewels in public. "Those spotty creeps on the corner jock hitch every time I walk by."

### keckchup

(kehk-tshup) *n.*: the sound of a nearby cat bringing up a fur ball. Syn. bootin' puss

### kermitt

(kuhr-miht) *n.*: chilling sensation in a human hand into which a toad or frog has just squirted whatever it is they squirt

### kiltatiltaphobia

(kihl-tah-till-tah-foh-bee-ah) *n.:* the terrifying awareness that an entirely unattractive, fully clothed male has an erection aimed at you

### knugget

(nuh-get) *n.:* astonishingly hard bone white chunk discovered in the course of chewing on sausage, hamburger, cheap ground meat in general

## lava lunch

(lah-vah-luhntsch) *n.:* the end
product of laughing through your
nose with your mouth full

## linger log

(ling-ghur lawg) *n.:* unit of human waste from unknown donor discovered by unsuspecting lid-lifter

## liprosy

(lip-ruh-see) *n.:* white bits, shreds, and threads of dry skin dangling from a chapped mouth

## malt down

(mawlt down) *n.:* the (potentially lethal) fumes of stale, scotch-saturated stink seeping from every pore of a recently awakened sot

## masticles

(mahs-tik-ils) *n. pl.:* clumps of petrified chewing gum adhering to surfaces, e.g., bottoms of school desks, movie theater seats; not infrequently found in children's hair

## meadow mine

(meh-dough myn) *n. rural:* cow pie so obviously old and solid as to tempt one to step on it; beneath its tissue-thin crust lurks a pudding of green putrescence

## molaroids

(mole-uhr-oydz) *n. pl.:* teeth marks pitting the stubby pencil you are handed when asked to sign for anything

### mucha joe

(muck-a jow) *n.:* puddle of cold coffee and clotted artificial creamer in bottom of cup. Compare: "java curdle"

### mucilingus

(myoo-syl-ing-guhs) *n.:* the act of passionately kissing someone who spent the afternoon licking envelopes

### muggy mitt

(mugh-ee mit) *n.:* hot, moist, slippery condition of teenage date's palm. Syn. slick paw, juvenile deliquescence (Obsolete)

## mush-toddle

(muhsh taw-dul) *n.:* the tentative, side-to-side gait of a child with a loaded diaper

## muskular

(mus-kyew-lahr) *adj.:* of or
pertaining to the spreading sweat
stain under the arms of suit coats,
sports jackets, etc.

## navelint

(nayv-el-int) *n.:* stuff that collects in
the belly button; smells funky, feels
gritty, tastes salty

# nerk

(nuhrk) *v.:* to bite (one's own) fart bubbles in the bathtub. *n.:* person who appears likely to indulge in this practice. "Louise is such a nerk!"

## nicotox

(nik-oh-tawks) *n.:* 1. the gas inhaled when the wrong end of a filter cigarette is accidentally lit. 2. the pervasive chemical stink caused by an unextinguished cigarette igniting all the other butts in the ashtray

## oozone

(ooh-zown) *n.:* droplets which dribble onto your head while you're walking down the street on a sunny day—air-conditioner drool, you *hope* . . .

## oral abscession

(oh-rahl ahb-sessh-yun) *n.:* the compulsion to prod (with tongue) at sores inside the mouth

## orange pukoe

(oh-ranj pyewk-oh) *n.:* dank, moldy nest of ancient foliage stuck to bottom of seldom used teapot

### over-boilage

(oh-vur boyl-idj) *n.:* sooty, lumpy
strata of petrified soup and gravy
spills encrusting the plumbing under
gas stove elements

### palmgrubs

(pom-gruhbz) *n. pl.:* strings of black
grease which materialize when an
individual of dubious hygiene rubs
his hands together

## pecker-boos

(pekh-ur booz) *n.:* the sort of gentlemen's swimming trunks which become transparent when wet, permitting bystanders an unwished-for glimpse of the contents

## phlegg

(fle-hg) *n.:* viscous string of albumen, unpleasant when occurring in scrambled eggs, utterly appalling in a nog

## phungo

(fung-go) *n.:* urban street game; requires hours of practice, split-second timing: Player blows his nose into the wind, then hand-swats the product onto the sidewalk

### pickled hearing
(pik-uld heering) *n.:* earwax, when taken orally

### piddlywinks
(pid-lee-win-x) *n. pl.:* tell-tale wet spots adorning the flies and upper trouser legs of gentlemen returning from the loo

### pigtrails
(pyg-traylz) *n. pl.:* slimy wet tracks left on the sidewalk behind dragged trash

### poinsitters

(poyn-sit-urz) *n. pl.:* bright red spots blossoming on the buttocks on or about the winter solstice

### polygrot

(pahl-ee-grawt) *adj.:* of or pertaining to/similar to the floor of a parrot's cage Syn. paratgleet

## polyurine

(paw-lee-yer-in) *n.:* liquid found in the bottom of kitchen garbage can whenever the bag is removed

## poopcorn

(poohp-korn) *n.:* maize kernels which survive the trip through the digestive tract to decorate turds

## porige

(pohr-idj) *n.:* greasy spots, lumps, or smears left on bathroom mirrors by zit-popping teens

## prepsterpod

(prep-stir-pod) *n.:* the pale gray, slick, and malodorous film which forms on a sockless foot enclosed in a Topsider

## psno

(pee-snow) *n.:* yellow snow (inedible)

## pubert

(pyu-burt) *n.:* single curled hair adhering to a bar of soap

# pupchuck

(puhp-tshuk) *n.:* dog vomit (edible, to dogs)

## queasy off

(kwee-zee awf) *n.:* crust of foul, greasy, crud-flecked foam in your oven, which means it is now partly clean. All you have to do is put your hands in there . . .

## quiltswoggle

(kwilt-swah-gul) *v.:* the sneaky midnight maneuver of using one's toes to lift the blanket at the foot of the bed and allow a fart to escape undetected

## quimania

(kwym-ayn-ee-ah) *n.:* addiction to the smell of girls' bicycle seats

## quimaniac

(kwym-ayn-ee-ahk) *n.:* person
afflicted with quimania (which See);
a normal adolescent male

## ratsnacks

(raht-snax) *n. pl.:* lumps of clotted
grease and other rotting black
foodstuffs adhering to the floor
under the fridge

## retch-a-sketch

(reh-tcha-skeh-tsh) *n.:* sidewalk art

### rhinestain

(ryn-stayn) *n.:* green and purple blotches left on the skin by cheap jewelry. "I'm going to wait a week before saying yes to Ted because I think this ring may give me rhinestain."

### ringburn

(ring-bern) *n.:* condition of the human fundament on the day after "pigging-out" on chili or curry

### rubber sement

(ruh-bur see-mehnt) *n.:* substance that keeps the pages of dirty books stuck together. Compare: "deweys"

## ruggage

(ruhg-edj) *n.:* the unbelievable knots of old hair, dust balls, nail clippings, lint, crumbs, dead bugs, and other filth one must occasionally extract from the innards of the carpet sweeper

## salime

(say-lime) *n.:* film of semitranslucent eye discharge accumulating on soft contact lens and impervious to chemical solutions, enzyme treatments, etc.

## scabble

(skah-bul) *n.:* children's game, consists of picking and flicking knee scabs

## scome

(s-kum) *n.:* sperm stains

## she shells

(shee shelz) *n. pl.:* plastic tampon applicators washed up on the beach

## shickstorm

(shik-storm) *n.:* shaving residue; surprisingly copious drifts of bristles clustered around sink and/or bath drains. Compare: "gilletinous"

## snorgasm

(snowr-gah-sum) *n.:* a sudden loud outburst of nasal noise by a sleeper — grounds for justifiable homicide by the waking partner in most states

## snot-weed factor

(snawt-weed fah-ktore) *n.:* the pollen count. Archaic/Obsolete

## spickle

(spik-ul) *n.:* yellowish foam which gathers in the corners of some people's mouths when they talk; sometimes accompanied by a midmouth yo-yo of extreme viscosity and hypnotic effect

## squattles

(skwah-tulz) *n.:* festoons of rear thigh cellulite displayed by hunkered-down matrons in shorts

### stashers

(stah-churz) *n. pl.:* food or mucus remnants stored for future reference in the moustache

### stemch

(stehmp-tch) *n.:* the nauseatingly fetid stink of vase water in which cut daisies have stood

## supercacafrowzylipstickup pychuckatrocious

(soo-pur-kaka-frowz-el-lip-stik-uhpee-tshuk-aht-roh-shus)

*adj.:* of or pertaining to the normal condition of a gas station toilet

## sweatch

(sweh-tsh) *n.:* perspiration, bitter
and metallic to the taste, which
accrues under watch bands


## swigarrest

(swig-ahr-est) *n.:* the precise
moment in time when you see the
cigarette butt in the beer bottle at
your lips

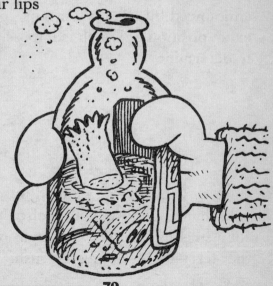

## tabbyocca

(tab-ee-oh-ka) *n.:* cat vomit

## termice

(tuhr-my-s) *n. pl.:* decomposing rodents between walls or floors, presence of which is customarily announced by olfactory means, exact position of which is impossible to determine

## terryuki

(tare-ee yuck-ee) *n.:* wadded-up, cold, hard wash rag with moist, sour-smelling center. "The sight of that terryuki is ruining my sushi."

### thesspit

(theh-spyt) *n.:* saliva sprayed into the eyes of audience members by Shakespearian actors. "I got Pacino's thesspit all over my good suit."

## tobacco-batique

(tow-bak-oh bah-teek) *n.:* abstract earth-tone pattern on floor around cuspidor

## togethernester

(too-geh-thur-ness-tur) *n.:* an especially fulgent specimen of passed gas which has been ripening under the sheets all night; literally a rude awakening for one's beloved. "Darling, a togethernester! You shouldn't have!"

## tom droolery

(tawm drew-lur-ee) *n.:* partial
contents of cocktail glass sloshed
onto fancy clothes or expensive
carpet in response to sally of wit at a
sophisticated party


## toobers

(two-berz) *n. pl.:* long neglected
potatoes in a corner of the pantry
which have begun to sprout.Syn.
slut-spuds

## toothpig

(too-th-pyg) *n.:* person who dislodges postprandial morsels from between molars, then eats them

## tuna smelt

(tune-ah smelt) *n.:* Friday's lunch box on Monday morning

## tuskies

(tuh-skeez) *n. pl.:* strands of hair extruding from the nostrils

## tutor juice

(toot-or joos) *n.:* amber substance composed of equal parts saliva and tobacco, ranging in color from urine-yellow to fecal-brown, which dribbles down the stem of the old professor's pungent pipe; staring agog at the droplet dangling from the bowl of the briar can result in loss of concentration, grade-points, lunch

## uglace

(ugh-lay-s) *n.:* slimy, grimy untied shoe string which has been dragged through rainy city streets

## underpiss

(uhn-duhr-pihs) *n.:* The pungent juice that drips down the walls and dribbles from the roof of all subterranean tunnels provided for pedestrians

## urban transpit

(er-bahn tranz-pit) *n.:* sinister puddle of unknown origin occupying the only empty seat on a city bus

## varicose drains

(vahr-ick-os dray-nz) *n. pl.:* condition in which the previous tenants left the plumbing; a clotted compost of hair, discarded sanitary aids, vegetable matter, bottle tops, birth control devices, etc., resulting in gross gurgling sound effects and brackish back-up

## verdish

(vuhr-dysh) *adj.*: of or related to or similar to the astonishing smell of asparagus eaters' pee pee

## vernal equinoxious

(vehr-nahl eek-win-awks-yus) *adj.*: pertaining to the putrid fecal reek of spring thaw at the dog run

## waggin trail

(wag-in trayl) *n.:* track left on carpet
by family dog after he has tucked his
back paws up behind his ears and
with his front paws dragged his
itchy ass across the room

## wainscoating

(wes-cot-ing) *n.*: petrified drifts of unthinkable grunge, occurring at baseboard, maddeningly inaccessible to vacuum cleaner nozzle

## wax-me-nots

(wacks-me-nawtz) *n.*: stray strands of pubic hair peeping from the crotch of a bathing suit

## willknots

(wil-notz) *n. pl.*: dingleberries which steadfastly resist attempts at removal by normal means

## witchkers

(whitsh-kurz) *n.:* your
grandmother's moustache

## writo-rooter

(ryt-oh-ruh-tur) *n.:* pencil or
ballpoint pen inserted in ear for
purposes of aural hygiene

### xerots

(zee-rahtz) *n. pl.:* smudges left on
the duplicating machine by waggish
co-worker's attempts to photocopy
his bare ass

## yuk-yuk-yuk

(iuhk-iuhk-iuhk) *v.:* to laugh so hysterically and continuously as to lose control over one's orifices and excretions

## yurk

(yerck) *v.:* to abort a belch; an unwholesome and unnatural act, causing severe jaw strain and resulting in "afterburp" (which See). Compare: "downchuck," "bumgulp"

## zapitos

(zahp-ee-tohz) *n.:* the crisp remains of recently electrocuted moths and/or other insects landing in the guacamole on the patio

## zen boogism

(zehn booh-giz-m) *n.:* the contented, trancelike state achieved by zealous nose pickers in public places